MOM! THE MONSTERS!

Written by
Liliana Cinetto

Illustrated by
Poly Bernatene

PaRragon

Bath · New York · Cologne · Melbourne · Delhi
Hong Kong · Shenzhen · Singapore · Amsterdam

For my children Sol, Juani y Flor,
because in fact they are the ones
who really protect me.

L.C.

For Matias and his curls!
And to Mom Paula, who protects
us from the monsters.

P.B.

This edition published by Parragon Books Ltd in 2015 and distributed by

Parragon Inc.
440 Park Avenue South, 13th Floor
New York, NY 10016
www.parragon.com

Published by arrangement with Meadowside Children's Books

Text © Liliana Cinetto 2011
Illustrations © Poly Bernatene 2011

ISBN 978-1-4748-1036-4

Printed in China

MOM! THE MONSTERS!

Written by
Liliana Cinetto

Illustrated by
Poly Bernatene

PaRragon

Bath • New York • Cologne • Melbourne • Delhi
Hong Kong • Shenzhen • Singapore • Amsterdam

Once upon a time, I was very, very afraid at night.
Terribly afraid.

So afraid that my hands
shook like this ...

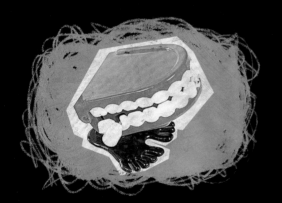

And my teeth
chattered like this ...

And my heart beat
like this ...

I was afraid because I thought that THEY were hiding in the dark. Hairy monsters with sharp teeth who smelled like dirty socks.

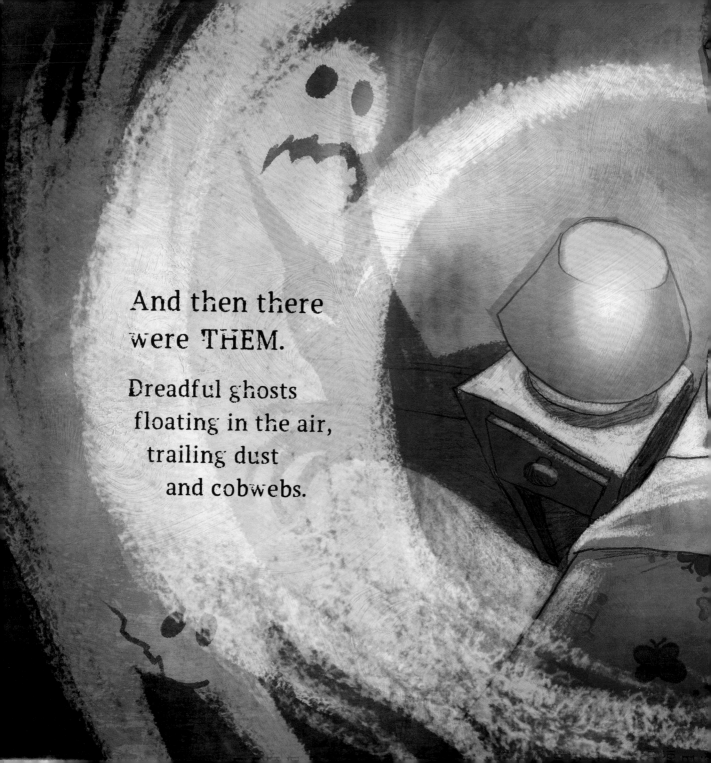

And then there were THEM.

Dreadful ghosts
floating in the air,
trailing dust
and cobwebs.

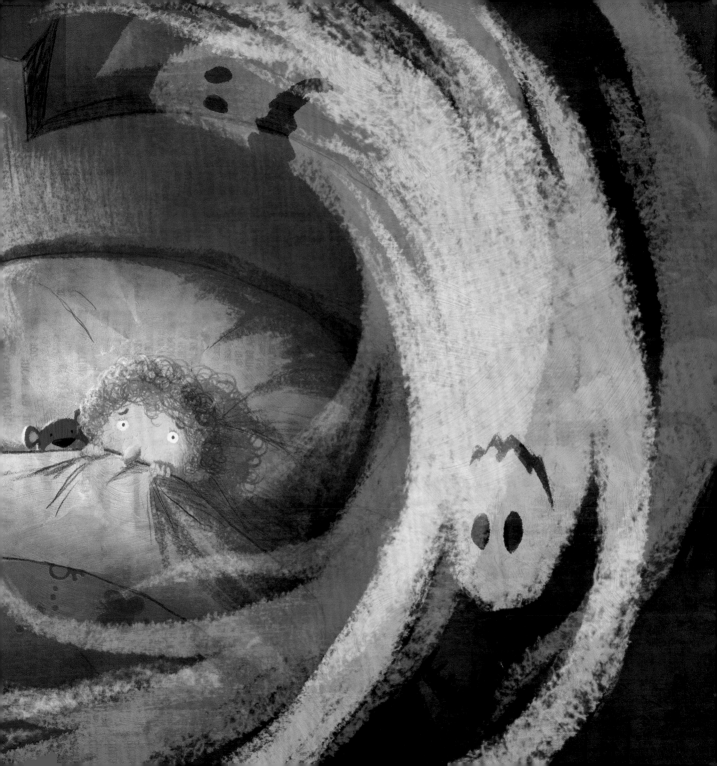

Or THEM.

Witches with messy
hair, and pointy hats,
and yellow eyes.

Or even THEM.

Huge ogres with huge hands, and huge
feet, and huge mouths full of
green drool.

I was sure that they wanted to catch me. Or turn me into a toad. Or eat me with a sprinkling of parsley. So, in the middle of the night, I'd shout:

"Moooooooom! The monsters!"

And Mom would put on the light, and sing songs to me until I went back to sleep.

And, in a dark corner, the monsters and the witches,
and the ghosts, and the ogres waited.
They did not move.

But they were watching me ....

Then, one day, Mom got tired of
always having to get up in the
middle of the night.
"You're a big boy now. You shouldn't
be afraid anymore."

"But Mom, the monsters ..."
"Monsters don't exist," she said, as she vacuumed under
my bed, sucking up the dust and some hairy monsters
(the ones with sharp teeth who smelled like dirty socks).

"What about the ghosts?" I asked.
"They don't exist either," she said, as she loaded
the washing machine with towels and sheets
and a few dreadful ghosts

(the ones who floated
about trailing dust
and cobwebs).

"But what about
the witches?" I asked.
"Not at all," she told me,
while she tidied up
the closet, straightening
the books and a few witches
(the ones with messy hair
and pointy hats and yellow eyes).

"And the
ogres?"
I wanted
to know.

"No way!" said Mom, as she swept the kitchen floor, brushing up breadcrumbs and bits of paper and a few huge ogres (the ones with huge hands, huge feet, and huge mouths full of green drool).

"Are you sure, Mom?
Are there really
no monsters?"

"They're just stories, dear!" she told me,
while she washed the dishes, and the monsters ...

... and ironed the sheets and the ghosts ...

And while she cleaned the furniture and the witches ...

And rested on the sofa with some comfy cushions and huge ogres.

That's why I'm not scared
of anything now.
Monsters, ghosts, witches,
and ogres don't come to my
bedroom anymore:
THEY are too afraid!

Because they know that their biggest
nightmare lives in my house ...

... my mom!

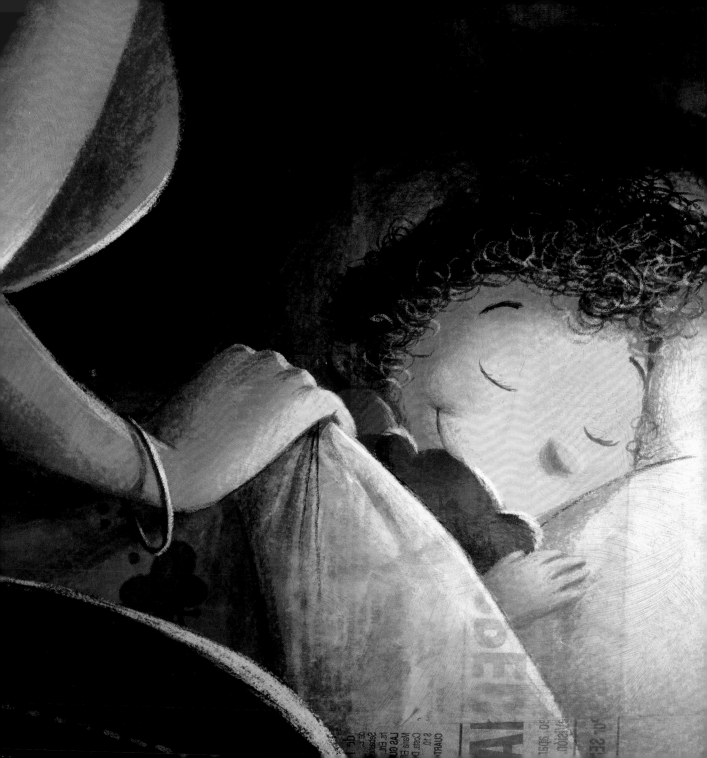